I Like, I Don't Like

Written by

ANNA BACCELLIERE

Illustrated by

ALE + ALE

EERDMANS BOOKS FOR YOUNG READERS

GRAND RAPIDS, MICHIGAN

I like shoes.

I like bricks.

I don't like bricks.

I don't like popcorn.

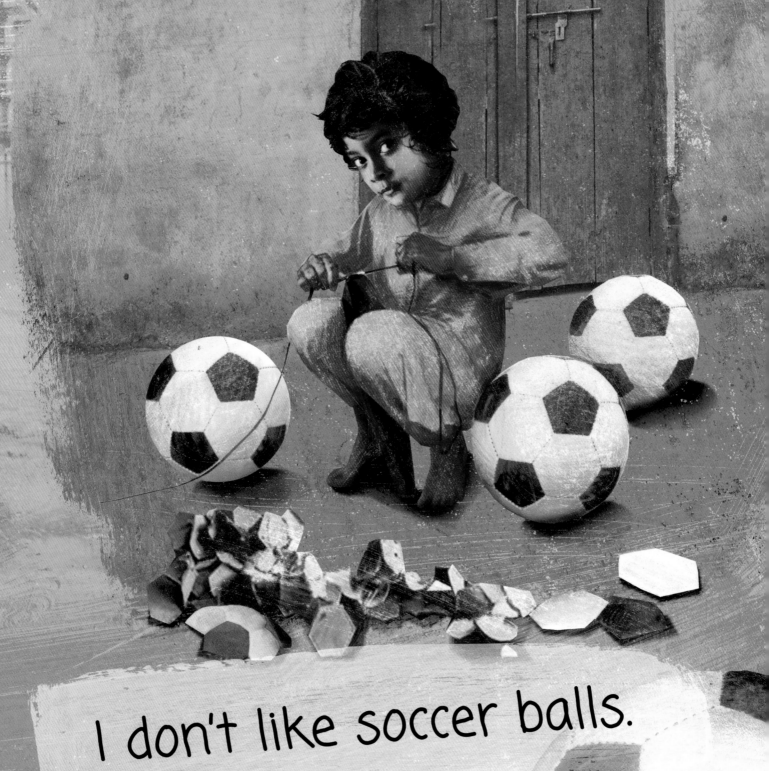

I don't like soccer balls.

I like rugs.

I don't like rugs.

I like rice.

I don't like music.

I don't like cars.

I like phones.

I like seashells.

I like flowers.

I don't like flowers.

What is playing?

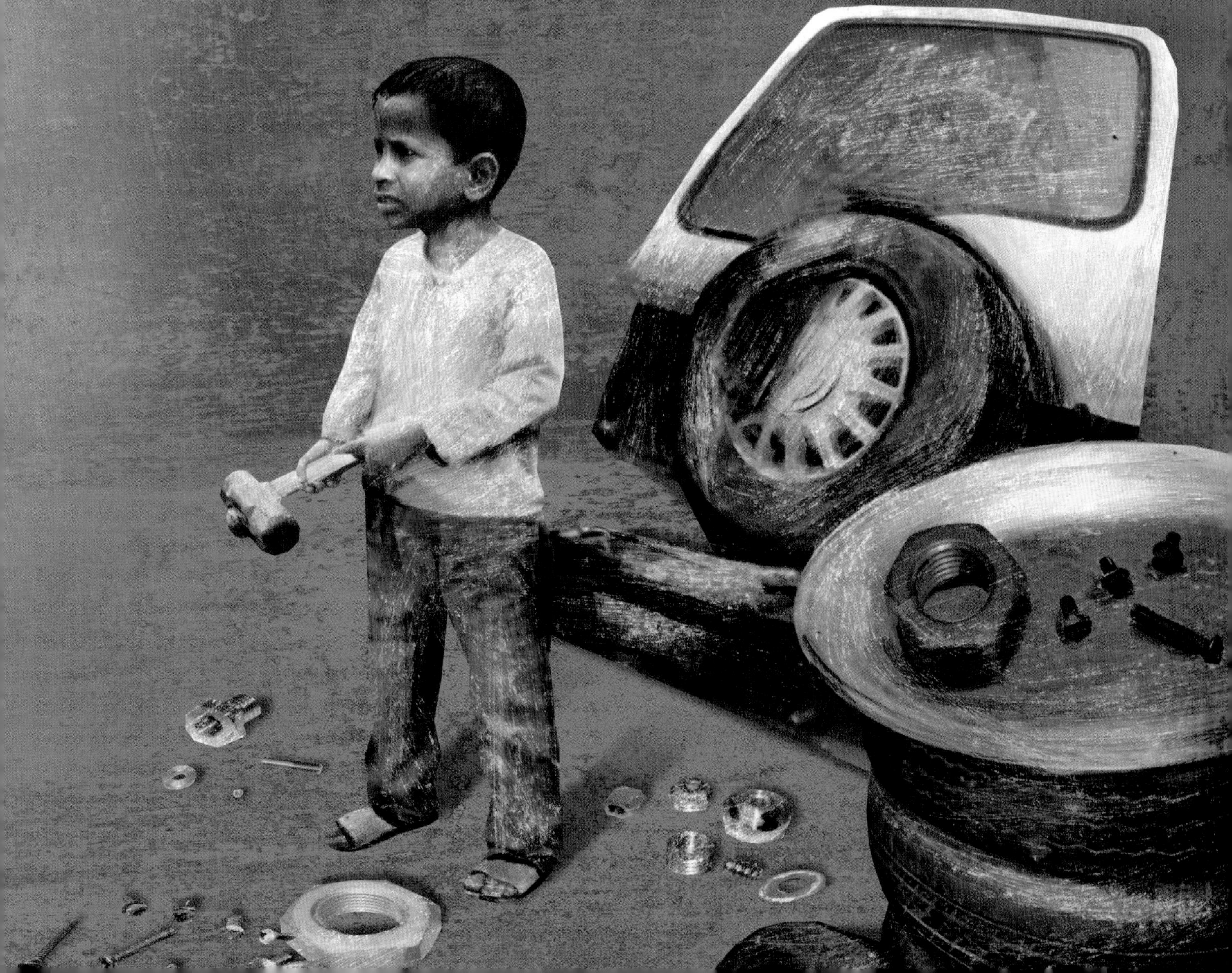

Poverty and Child Labor

Child labor and poverty are serious issues throughout the world. People who live in poverty have limited choices and opportunities. Poverty is the single greatest cause of child labor — impoverished families often need their children's income for survival. The employment of children is widely considered immoral and exploitative because it interferes with children's ability to attend school and deprives them of their childhood.

There are many organizations dedicated to reducing global poverty, including the United Nations. Even so, childhood poverty remains prevalent. More than 16 million children in the United States — 22% of all U.S. children — live below the poverty line, and many children throughout the world must work to help their families.

Convention on the Rights of the Child

In 1989, the United Nations introduced a human rights treaty called the Convention on the Rights of the Child. The Convention establishes and protects the unalienable rights of children, such as freedom of speech and religion, protection against abuse, the right to play and receive an education, and the right to have a life of dignity. Every nation that ratifies the Convention is bound to it by international law. Currently, 196 countries have ratified it, including every member of the United Nations, with the exception of the United States.

How Can I Help?

Fortunately, there are many opportunities for you to help fight poverty, both in your community and throughout the world. Fundraisers and monetary donations can go a long way, but there are plenty of other ways you can get involved. Check out the following organizations for ideas about how you can make a difference:

Amnesty International is committed to fighting the abuse of human rights worldwide. Learn more at www.amnesty.org.

UNICEF works to promote the rights and improve the lives of children throughout the world. Learn more at www.unicef.org.

You can also look for organizations right in your community that focus on poverty-related issues such as hunger or homelessness — and getting involved with family and friends can help you to have an even greater impact.

Anna Baccelliere published her first children's book in 2004. Since then she has written numerous books for children and young adults and won several literary awards. She currently lives in Italy, where she teaches and conducts creative writing workshops for adults and children.

Ale + Ale is the creative team of Italian artists Alessandro Lecis and Alessandra Panzeri, who have been working together since 2000. Although they fantasize about creating collages in a spaceship orbiting earth, they can actually be found at their studio in Paris. Visit their website at www.ale-ale.net.

A Vittoria, profumo in boccio del mio domani.
— A. B.

This English edition published in 2017 under license from edizioni ARKA
by Eerdmans Books for Young Readers,
an imprint of Wm. B. Eerdmans Publishing Co.
2140 Oak Industrial Dr. NE, Grand Rapids, Michigan 49505
www.eerdmans.com/youngreaders

Original Italian text by Anna Baccelliere · Illustrations by Ale + Ale
Original Italian edition © edizioni ARKA - Milano/Italy

17 18 19 20 21 22 23   9 8 7 6 5 4 3 2 1

Manufactured at Tien Wah Press in Malaysia

ISBN 978-0-8028-5480-3

A catalog record of this book is available from the Library of Congress.

Display type set in Amatic SC · Text type set in Coming Soon and Liberation Serif